MORNING CREEK ELEMENTARY SCHOOL
10025 MORNING CREEK DRIVE SO.
SAN DIEGO, CA 92128

CAROLINA HERRERA
International Fashion Designer

CAROLINA HERRERA
International Fashion Designer

By Janet Riehecky

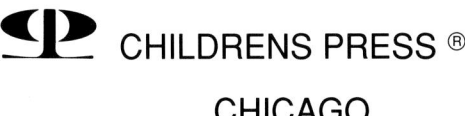

CHILDRENS PRESS ®
CHICAGO

PHOTO CREDITS

AP/Wide World Photos — 19 (right)

Gamma Liaison — ©Marc Karzen, cover

Photographs provided by Carolina Herrera — 1, 5, 6 (3 photos), 7, 8 (2 photos), 9, 10, 12 (2 photos), 13, 14, 16, 19 (left), 20 (2 photos), 21 (2 photos), 22, 24 (2 photos), 25, 26 (2 photos), 27, 28, 29 (2 photos), 31; ©Chris Alexander for *Interview* magazine, 2; Debeers Diamonds "Women of Quality" Exhibition 1984, 3; ©Foto Cervi, 11; DeVries Public Relations, 17 (4 photos), 18 (2 photos); Official White House Photograph, 23

For my wonderful husband, John: Thank you for your love, patience, and confidence in me.

Project Manager: E. Russell Primm III
Design and Electronic Composition: Biner Design
Photo Researcher: Judy Feldman

Library of Congress Cataloging-in-Publication Data

    Carolina Herrera : international fashion designer / by Janet Riehecky.
    p. cm. — (Picture story biography)
    Summary: Follows the life of the prominent dress designer, from her childhood in Venezuela through her growing interest in fashion to her current success in design.
    ISBN 0-516-04178-9
    1. Herrera, Carolina, 1939– —Juvenile literature. 2. Fashion designers—United States—Biography—Juvenile literature. [1. Herrera, Carolina, 1939– . 2. Fashion designers.] I. Title. II. Series: Picture-story biographies.

TT505.H44R54 1991   90-28886
746.9'2'092—dc20   CIP
[B]   AC
[92]

Copyright © 1991 by Childrens Press®, Inc.
All rights reserved. Published simultaneously in Canada.
Printed in the United States of America.
1 2 3 4 5 6 7 8 9 10 R 99 98 97 96 95 94 93 92 91

When people describe the clothes that Carolina Herrera designs, they use one word over and over again — "elegant." Nancy Reagan wears Carolina Herrera evening dresses for private dinner parties in Beverly Hills. When Caroline Kennedy needed the perfect wedding dress, she turned to Carolina Herrera.

Carolina Herrera with Caroline Kennedy Schlossberg at her wedding in July 1986.

Carolina Herrera is one of the world's leading dress designers. As a little girl growing up in Venezuela, she never thought of being a dress designer. In fact, having any career never seemed likely.

Maria Carolina Pacanins de Herrera was born on January 8, 1939, to an important and wealthy family in

(top left) Carolina's maternal grandmother at age 18; (bottom left) Carolina's mother, Maria Cristina Nino-Passios de Pacanins in 1944; (right) Carolina's father, Guillermo Pacanins-Acevedo, 1932.

Caracas, Venezuela. Her father was commander of the Venezuelan Air Force. He also served as the governor of Caracas. Her mother was a society hostess.

As a young girl, Carolina lived in a large, beautiful house surrounded by gardens. She rode horses, took tennis lessons, and lived a comfortable life. Her life, however, was very restricted. She and her three sisters were always watched closely by a Hungarian governess. The girls were raised to believe that they would marry, have

Carolina dressed as Snow White at age 4 in her grandmother's home in Caracas.

(left) Carolina and her mother traveling in the south of France in 1944; (right) Carolina's mother in 1968.

babies, and serve their husbands. Carolina never questioned her future. But from the time she was young, Carolina was preparing for her future career.

As a girl, Carolina loved fashion. She saw well-dressed people in beautifully made clothes. She soon developed an eye for what looked right and what didn't. She experimented with fabrics and styles. She also designed clothes for her dolls.

Although a private dressmaker came to their home, Carolina's mother and grandmother also traveled to Paris to buy clothes. When Carolina was thirteen, her grandmother took her to see a fashion show. There she met Cristobal Balenciaga, one of the world's greatest clothing designers. Carolina was thrilled by high fashion. Each time she returned to Paris, she loved it more.

Carolina (left), her mother (right), and her younger sister Alexandra (center) in 1955.

As a teenager, Carolina expressed strong opinions about what she wanted to wear. She longed to look older and more sophisticated, so she put on fake eyelashes and red lipstick. Unfortunately, her family did not understand. Her father wouldn't allow her to continue.

Carolina wanted to look different from everyone else. When it was allowed, she tried new and different styles. If everyone else was wearing short skirts, she wanted hers to be long.

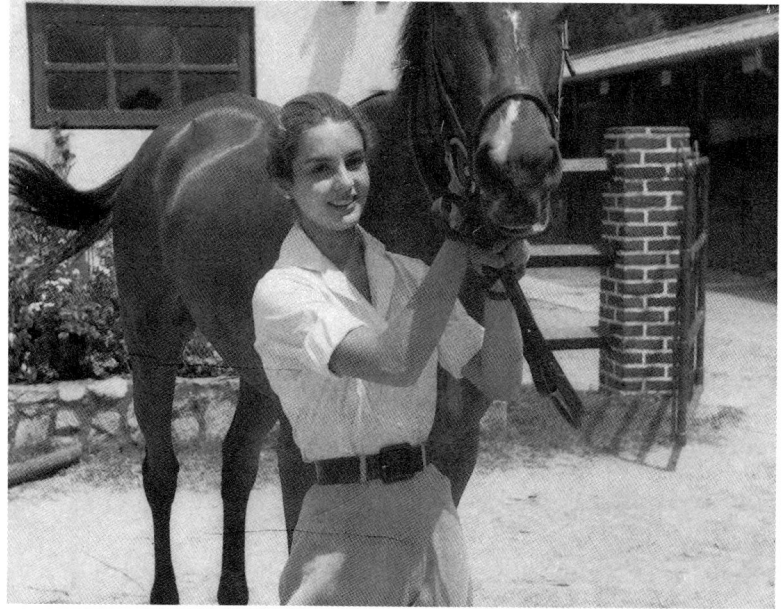

Carolina with her horse Balaclava in 1955.

Carolina in Caracas at age 15.

Although Carolina liked the unusual, there were times when she preferred the traditional. At age fifteen, she made her debut in Venezuelan society. She looked like a princess in a white ball gown from Paris.

As a young woman, Carolina wore clothes from famous designers such as Valentino, Christian Dior, Yves Saint Laurent, and Giorgio Armani. She married and focused her attention on her husband and her house. Soon, she also had two daughters, Mercedes and Ana Luisa, to care for.

Unfortunately, this marriage proved to be unhappy for Carolina. Even though it caused her great pain, after eight years, she was divorced.

In 1968, Carolina married Reinaldo Herrera, a wealthy Venezuelan landowner. She and Reinaldo had been friends since childhood. They have two daughters, Carolina and Patricia.

(left) Carolina and Reinaldo at their wedding, September 20, 1968, in Caracas. Carolina designed her own wedding dress. (right) Mrs. Herrera and her two-year-old daughter Carolina at Hacienda la Vega in 1971.

Carolina and Reinaldo at Hacienda la Vega, Caracas, in 1973.

    Carolina and Reinaldo moved in international society. They divided their time between New York City and the family mansion in Caracas. They also made frequent trips to Europe. Carolina enjoyed choosing her clothing from the world's best designers. But she also began designing her own clothes.

    When Carolina got an idea for a new dress, she made a sketch of it and took it to her dressmaker. Together, they

Carolina models a jeweled gown at home in 1973.

turned Carolina's ideas into gowns. Carolina's friends loved the dresses she created. Several friends convinced her to design clothes for them.

In 1972, Carolina was named to the International Best Dressed List. She was named to this list every year for the next ten years. She then retired to the Best Dressed Hall of Fame. Frequently, the clothes that caught everyone's eye were of her own design.

Friends and family began to encourage Carolina to do more with her designs. Diana Vreeland, editor of *Vogue* magazine, suggested that she develop her own line of clothes. The timing seemed right to Carolina. She was not as surprised as she once would have been. Starting her own business suddenly seemed possible. The world no longer frowned upon women having careers. Carolina's daughters were no longer young. Reinaldo gave lots of encouragement and support.

Carolina went to work. She created twenty dresses in Caracas and returned to New York City. The enthusiasm shown there encouraged her to go ahead. With money from Armando de Armas, head of a South American publishing company, she opened her own company in New York, Carolina Herrera, Ltd.

In 1981, Carolina presented her first collection in New York City. The fashion world was at first skeptical.

A photo of Carolina from her first press kit in 1981.

On this page are examples of fashions that Carolina created for her premiere spring and summer collection in 1982.

Many thought Carolina was simply a rich woman amusing herself with fashion. Others were convinced that high fashion designers had to be men.

But the Carolina Herrera Collection impressed even her strongest critics. Words such as "marvelous" and "sensational" didn't seem to be strong enough for their excitement. The department store Saks Fifth Avenue immediately bought the entire

Carolina Herrera's fall and winter 1982 collection featured exciting new fashions, including a dress in her favorite polka dot pattern.

collection. Their decision was a good one. Carolina's collection became a best seller for them.

Today, Carolina's life revolves around her business. She travels the world as she has always done. Now, however, she travels promoting her designs. Her home is New York City. When she is there, she walks each morning to her East 57th Street offices. On one such walk, she met a visually

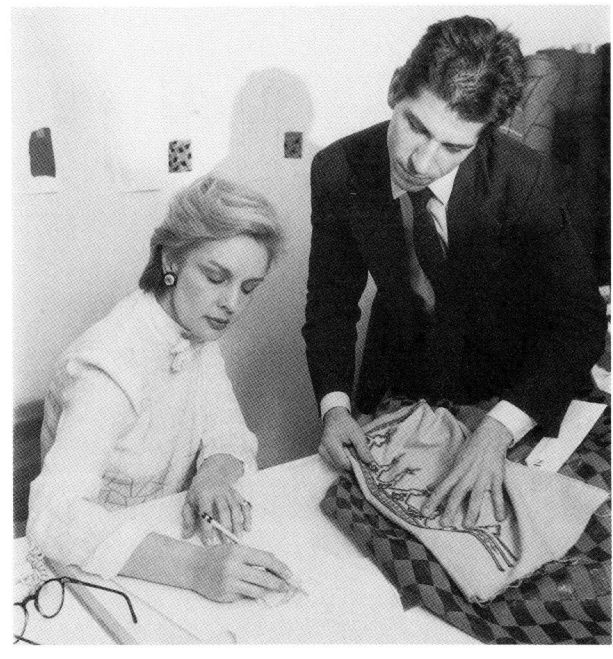

(left) An outfit from the fall and winter 1983 collection; (right) Carolina consults with an assistant on the fall designs.

impaired man crossing a busy street. They started chatting. Carolina discovered that the man owned an office supply business. To this day, Carolina's company does much business with her friend. He visits often, taking the company's orders in braille.

The Herrera look is simple, but elegant. Carolina dislikes ruffles and bows. She thinks only the best materials should be used. She loves

padded shoulders and believes they help a woman look her best.

Carolina refuses to overload a dress with details as some designers do. Her dresses usually have only a single, "wonderful" detail. Carolina's favorite pattern is black-and-white polka dots. She says polka dots are "happy."

Whatever the style, Carolina insists that her clothing must be comfortable. Part of elegance is how a person

Examples of clothing from Carolina Herrera's 1986 through 1989 collections.

moves. A woman can't move with elegance in an uncomfortable dress. Carolina experiments on herself. She drapes fabric around herself. If it feels awkward, she changes it. Carolina says she only makes dresses she herself would wear.

Carolina no longer chooses her clothes from other designers. She feels she should wear only her own designs. Many people have said Carolina is her own best model. Now in her fifties, she is petite with large brown eyes, perfect skin, and silky blond hair worn swept up or back.

Carolina Herrera at home in New York City, 1990.

In 1985, Carolina Herrera met President Ronald Reagan.

Carolina still leads an active social life, but now it's part of her business. She goes to concerts, art shows, the opera, and charity events. Everywhere she goes she watches what people are wearing. She looks at shape, color, and interesting use of materials.

Each collection of clothes that Carolina has made since 1981 has been a tremendous success. Her company, Carolina Herrera, Ltd., began with only twelve employees. Today, Carolina employs 111 people.

In August 1986, Carolina brought out another line of clothes under the "CH" label. These clothes are designed for women who can't afford to spend $1,500 for a dress. Carolina also has a bridal collection, which she began in October 1987. In August 1989, she started a line of sportswear. A perfume with her name, packaged in a black-and-white polka-dot box, was

(left) An example of the clothing Carolina creates for her CH label of clothing. (right) A bridal gown from the fall/winter of 1990.

Carolina walks down the runway after her successful spring and summer 1991 fashion show.

introduced in April 1988. A fragrance for men will be available in September 1991.

Carolina Herrera has recently been ranked as one of the top twenty-seven designers in the world. Yet, Carolina has not lost touch with the values on which she was raised.

Carolina loves fashion, but fashion comes after family. She recently told a Boston newspaper, "My husband and

(above) Carolina works on sketches in her New York office; (right) Seamstresses bring to reality Carolina's fashion ideas.

my four daughters are my first career. Fashion is my second career."

Carolina keeps her family very close. She relies on their support and encouragement, asks their opinions, and is proud of their achievements. Her oldest daughter, Mercedes, has three sons, and Carolina adores being a grandmother. She makes a point of spending August with them.

Her family, in turn, is very proud of her. The girls love the fact that their mother has a career—something

Dress dummies are used to fit a new design for the 1991 resort wear collection.

Carolina's Hungarian governess would never have understood. Most importantly, Reinaldo is very supportive. Carolina doesn't hesitate to express how much she needs him. She has said, "My husband understands my ambitions. I discuss all my ideas with him. He is not involved in my business, but he has great taste and great style."

Because family is so important to Carolina, she makes certain that her

Mr. and Mrs. Herrera at home in New York City, 1990.

(left) Carolina and her first grandson Robert Mendoza in 1983; (above) Alfonso maintains a regular work schedule along with Carolina in her New York City offices.

employees are made to feel like family members. Carolina brings her dog, Alfonso, to work with her every day. Her grandsons are frequent visitors to the office. At Christmas, the employees at Carolina Herrera, Ltd., donate gifts to needy children instead of giving gifts among themselves.

For all her fame and glittering lifestyle, Carolina Herrera is happiest when life is simple. Basically she is a shy and very private person. She loves to spend evenings at home with her family, her dog, and her cat, Sebastian. Carolina also loves to read. Still she would never think of giving up her business. Carolina treasures her success and is proud of the name she has made for herself.

Carolina Herrera has received many awards for the beautiful clothes she has designed. But the award that pleases her most is the reaction of the women who buy her clothes and the enthusiasm of her biggest fans — her family.

The Herrera family at home in New York City, 1990.

CAROLINA HERRERA

1939	January 8 — Born in Caracas, Venezuela
1944	Debuts in Venezuelan society
1968	September 20 — Marries Reinaldo Herrera in Caracas
1972–1981	Carolina Herrera named to International Best Dressed List for ten years in a row; retired to the Best Dressed Hall of Fame.
1981	Carolina presents her first fashion collection in New York City
1986	August — Began the "CH" label of clothing
1987	October — Debut of first bridal collection
1988	April — Carolina Herrera perfume is released
1989	August — Carolina Herrera brought out her first sportswear collection
1991	September — Carolina Herrera's men's fragrance is available

INDEX

Alfonso (Carolina's dog), 29
Armani, Giorgio, 11
Armas, Armando de, 16
Balaclava (Carolina's horse), 10
Balenciaga, Cristobal, 9
Best Dressed Hall of Fame, 14
bridal collection, 24
Caracas, Venezuela, 6, 16
Carolina Herrera, Ltd., 16, 23, 29
"CH" collection, 24
Dior, Christian, 11
fashion design, 5, 6, 8, 13, 25
fragrances, 24, 25
France, 8
Hacienda la Vega (Caracas), 13
Herrera, Carolina (daughter), 12
Herrera, Patricia (daughter), 12
Herrera, Reinaldo (husband),12, 13, 16, 25, 28, 31
International Best Dressed List, 14
Laurent, Yves Saint, 11
Mendoza, Roberto (grandson), 29
New York City, 13, 16, 19
Nino-Passios de Pacanins, Maria Cristina (mother), 6
Pacanins-Acevedo, Guillermo (father), 6
Paris, 9, 11
Reagan, Nancy, 5
Reagan, Ronald, 23
Saks Fifth Avenue (department store), 18
Schlossberg, Caroline Kennedy, 5
Sebastian (Carolina's cat), 30
sportswear, 24
Valentino, 11
Venezuelan Air Force, 7
Venezuelan society, 11
Vogue (magazine), 15
Vreeland, Diana, 15
wedding dresses, 5

ABOUT THE AUTHOR

Janet Riehecky has always loved books. In fact, she says she'd rather give up breathing than give up reading. She decided to become a writer when she was ten years old and has been writing ever since.

Ms. Riehecky attended Illinois Wesleyan University where she studied to become a teacher. She spent five years as a high school English teacher and also completed two Master's degrees: one in Speech Communication at Illinois State University and one in English literature at Northwestern University. Ms. Riehecky is active in her church and has participated in various dramatic groups. She is married and has a son, Patrick. Ms. Riehecky loves writing for children. She is particularly proud of having won the 1988 Summit Award for children's nonfiction. She has published fifty-six books for children and plans to keep them coming!